COLD KISSER

COLD KISSER

Edgar J. Hyde

CCP

© 1997 Children's Choice Publications Ltd

First Printed 1997, reprinted 1999 (twice)
Creepers and Edgar J. Hyde are Registered Trademarks of
Children's Choice Publications Ltd.

Text supplied by Edgar J. Hyde

ISBN 1 90201 205 4

Printed and bound in the UK

Contents

Chapter 1

Tommy McDonald was what his classmates called "ordinary". He didn't hang out with the tough guys and he didn't have girls queuing up to ask him out on dates.

"I'm only thirteen! There's plenty of time for all that," he'd reply, when being teased by people like George Borden. George was only thirteen too, but he had kissed five girls! At least! Anyway, that's what he said.

"You got any witnesses to these kisses George?" Tommy would say.

"Witnesses – I prefer to kiss girls in private, not for a bunch of people to stand and cheer!"

"Well, how do I know you're not making it all up?"

"Just ask Lisa, or Lynsey or Jane . . . need I go on?"

"Okay, okay," Tommy would reply, knowing full well that he'd never ask Lisa, Lynsey or any other girl if she'd been kissed by George.

Tommy was feeling left out and George's confidence with girls made him feel childish by comparison.

Tommy was dreading the first year's end of term school disco. This would be the first disco for all those in Tommy's school year to celebrate – if that's the right word – completing the first year at the intimidating Moorbourne High School.

Being a quiet sort, Tommy had left all the mischief to the other boys in his class. He'd watched, with little interest, as they fought with each other and tried to impress – or even kiss – the girls. He'd also watched as the rougher boys and girls tried to see who could be cheekiest to the teachers. Some of these pupils seemed to think the point of school was to do your best not to be taught anything at all and to disrupt the class so that no-one else could learn either.

Tommy preferred to work hard, even do his homework and pass tests! The other boys often wondered what was wrong with him. Luckily for Tommy he was nearly 1.8 metres tall, despite only being thirteen.

On the few occasions any of the tough guys, like Ronnie Ryan, picked a fight with him, Tommy would fight back for all he was worth. Even though he lost the few fights he had, the Ronnie Ryans of the school eventually decided it was more trouble than it was worth to pick on Tommy.

Tommy wasn't the cleverest in his class. He had to work hard for his pass marks. But he did work hard. He wanted to be a reporter for a big newspaper when he left school and knew he needed qualifications. Fighting, teasing girls, detentions – these were for the clowns like Ronnie Ryan. Nothing was going to distract Tommy from his aim in life. Nothing.

Tommy lived only a street away from the school. George Borden used to be his next door neighbour until George's dad had got a new job and his family moved out of town to the suburbs. George was one of the boys who got the school bus home, and this gave him plenty of time to share after-school gossip with Tommy when they sat beside each other as they did in the English lessons.

"George," said Tommy after English one day, "You should be a ventriloquist when you leave school."

"Why?"

"Because, all through the English lesson you talked nonstop. I'm sure Mrs Gray heard your voice, but she never saw your lips move."

"Of course not," said George proudly "I practice in front of the mirror every night – when you're doing your homework, I suppose!"

"What for?"

"Because I never get to see you apart from in English. You never come out after school. You spend all your breaks in the library. You should live for now not for the future, then I wouldn't have to do all the talking. Then you might do things worth talking about."

"What, like kissing girls, running around after school with a football . . . great, eh? Don't you ever worry about the future, or what you might do after school?" enquired Tommy.

"Yeah, after school I'm taking Maggie Allen down to the park," replied George.

"No, I mean after, after school – when you're sixteen or eighteen, when you finally grow up – what are you going to be?" persisted Tommy.

"A ventriloquist – and 'cos you've nothing useful to say you'd make a great dummy!"

Tommy looked round at George as George decided to make himself scarce.

"See you tomorrow, Tommy," said George as he ran off to catch the school bus home. George was smiling and Tommy found it hard not to smile back.

"See you tomorrow, you nutter," shouted Tommy.

Chapter 2

"Now," said Miss Sharpe, over the din as class 1B settled into their chairs at tutorial.

Tommy sat on his own with a vacant seat beside him at tutorial. The desks were set out as follows: three long columns of desks were stretched from the front of the classroom to the back. Each column had five double desks, one behind the other. So most pupils sat beside another boy or girl. Tommy sat at the middle desk in the row nearest the large windows. The double desk behind him was completely empty, and Ronnie Ryan sat at the desk behind the empty one.

Ronnie was considered such a bad influence

that he sat on his own at most classes, always at the back. Most teachers appeared to have given up on him and decided to seat him as far away from the main learning action as possible. Unknown to the teachers, this merely gave Ronnie a great opportunity to stock up with paper bullets. Ronnie would take the ink part out of his biro pen and put the point end into his mouth. Then he'd put a bit of crumpled up paper, which he called his bullet, into the other end of the pen. Throughout most lessons, pupils that Ronnie didn't like, and that was most of them, would feel a slight sting on the back of their heads. They all knew that the cause of this annoyance was Ronnie and his paper bullets. But, the code of silence, which exists in all classrooms and forbids too much cooperation with teachers, was always at work. So the teachers were unaware of this particular vice of Ronnie's.

"Now," said Miss Sharpe, again, trying to live up to her name, "I want silence right now!" Gradually the rumblings and mutterings died down and Miss Sharpe could be heard. The pupils could see a beautiful girl standing beside Miss Sharpe at the blackboard, looking a little nervous, obviously waiting to be introduced.

"Before I read out the register, I'd like to introduce a new pupil. This is Sally Anne Dickens."

A few wolf whistles went up from the boys in the room. The girl called Sally Anne Dickens blushed. Her red face contrasted dramatically with her beautiful long straight blond hair, which was down to her waist. She was very tall, taller certainly than any other girl in the class. She was immaculately dressed and looked every inch the young lady. But, Tommy could sense that the girl was feeling very embarrassed and probably wanted to be sitting anonymously at a desk, not standing up in front of the class as the new pupil, an awful tag for anyone thought Tommy, especially someone who is shy!

Tommy realised that he felt attracted to Sally Anne. What boy wouldn't?

Miss Sharpe had finished the introductions and now asked Sally Anne to sit down at one of the vacant desks.

Tommy's heart beat faster as she walked up to, he thought, the vacant desk behind him.

"Oh no," thought Tommy, "sit somewhere else, please!" Although he had decided she was the first girl he really fancied, she made him so nervous that he really wished she would sit somewhere else entirely.

Tommy tried not to notice her as she got closer to his desk, then closer. Tommy's head was face down as he pretended to be engrossed in his jotter. But he was aware of her as she reached his desk. He waited for her to keep walking to the desk behind his. But she'd stopped. Then Tommy realised that she was looking at the vacant seat beside him!

Surely she would choose to sit at a double desk all to herself rather than share one with Tommy who was, after all, a stranger! But she was still standing beside him. He felt the full stare of all the class as they turned round to see where Sally Anne was going to sit. Then she spoke.

"Excuse me," she said.

Tommy's beetroot red face looked up and said, "Y-Y-Yes?"

"Is anyone sitting here?" she said softly.

"Er . . ."

"No Sally Anne," interrupted Miss Sharpe. "No-one is sitting there, I'm sure Tommy will move his school bag off that chair for you, won't you Tommy?"

"Of course," said Tommy, trying to recover from the embarrassment. "Of course, please, sit down," he said removing his school bag. But he hadn't fastened it properly that morning and all his books, pens, protractors, compass' and rulers fell out all over the floor. He bent under the desk to pick them up.

Then he heard George shout from the front of the classroom, "He's looking up her skirt." The class erupted in laughter. Tommy was now dripping with sweat, red as a pillar box and utterly ruffled. On hearing George's embarrassing joke, he tried to stand up quickly, forgetting that he was under his desk. The loud thud of Tommy's head hitting the underside of the desk produced another series of loud laughs from his classmates.

"That's enough," said Miss Sharpe, trying not to laugh. "Really, Tommy, can't you pick them up later?" Tommy wanted the ground to open up and swallow him right away. The laughter was dying down. Sally Anne had sat down beside him.

"Why me?" wondered Tommy. Miss Sharpe was walking back over to her desk to read the register out. Sally Anne hadn't appeared to be embarrassed at all. Perhaps she was glad that Tommy had unwittingly stolen the show and thus distracted attention away from her. But Tommy was sure when she caught his eye as she sat down, she smiled at him.

That was the first lesson of the term that Tommy could not properly remember. It was the first time he had not heard one word. In fact when the bell rang for the end of the lesson, Tommy was so shell shocked, he wondered if he'd been there at all.

Chapter 3

"What's she like, Tommy?" muttered George at English lesson later that day, in his best ventriloquist style. No answer.

"Come on, she's gorgeous. What's she like?" he persisted.

Still silence.

"Oh, here we go again. Tommy the dumb struck dummy with nothing to say. The most beautiful girl in the school decides to sit next to him and he'd still have nothing to say. Will I do both parts, Tommy? 'Well George,'" said George, imitating Tommy's deep voice, "' it's like this, I'm full of animal magnetism – girls can't resist me . . .'"

"Shut up, George," snapped Tommy angrily.

"Tommy, I'm joking but I tell you, if you're not interested in kissing Sally Anne, that's just as well 'cos you'd have to join a queue a mile long – with me at the front of it!" said George, laughing without moving his lips. Tommy said nothing.

Tommy didn't go to the library that morning break. He'd decided to go looking for Sally Anne. Not to talk to – no, nothing as brave as that, but just to look at her. She was pretty. He couldn't get her out of his mind.

When George saw Tommy in the playground at break, he broke off from his game of football to talk to him.

"You all right, Tommy?" he asked.

"Yeah, why shouldn't I be?" Tommy said emphatically.

"All right, all right, you look lost, that's all."

They saw Sally Anne talking to some of the girls from class over at the tuck shop queue.

"Let's go and introduce ourselves," said George, walking over to where Sally Anne was.

"What – what'll we say?" asked Tommy nervously.

"You say what you're good at saying, Tommy – nothing. When it comes to girls you're the dummy remember?" replied George.

Was George going to set up a date for Tommy with Sally Anne? Did he have a master plan worked out to bring these two soul mates together, wondered Tommy? Soul mates, thought Tommy, he wondered if there was really such a thing. The more he thought of Sally Anne, the more he said to himself "Okay, so now I'm interested in girls. Now what?"

As they approached the group of girls that included Sally Anne, Tommy felt his nerves ease. Now that he'd admitted to himself that he liked her, all he had to do was talk to her – gulp! He panicked.

"You do the talking, genius," he pleaded to George.

"Okay – I'm going to."

George had no idea that Tommy fancied Sally

Anne. George was going to do the talking because he fancied Sally Anne too.

"I'll make a spare seat beside me in class if you like," he said to Sally Anne.

"No, no," she blushed, shocked at George's up-front opening line.

"It's okay, really."

Tommy was livid, his best friend, only real friend, was talking to his girl.

"Really," George persisted, "I'll tie up Jimmy Leach, who sits beside me and leave him in the toilets. You and me have lots to talk about, sweetheart."

Sally Anne was mildly amused. George was obviously charming and harmless. But she really wanted Tommy to be the one making the moves, after all, that's why she'd sat down beside him at tutorial. She'd seen him through the crowd as the class arrived that morning. He was tall like her. She felt embarrassed looking down at boys like George. It made her feel old. She was only thirteen after all.

But Tommy had no idea what she was thinking. And because Tommy was silent, Sally Anne thought he wasn't interested. He must be here just to back up George, she thought.

"Can I buy you lunch sometime?" said George in his best American accent.

"Can you buy me lunch?" she repeated, amazed. She continued, "You mean the Ritz is nearby?"

"No, not really." George was a bit put out. I'll do the jokes he thought. "What about we share my sandwiches at lunchtime?"

"Only if you have smoked salmon and caviar," she joked.

"Great," said George, "I'll bring the champagne – or as its known in these parts – diet coke!"

"Dinner hall at 12.30?" she asked, almost disinterestedly.

"Done."

"See you then, big spender," she laughed.

"That's how its done," grinned George as he saw Tommy looking at him. "What's wrong pal, don't you want to learn how to get girls? I'm not even charging you for the lesson!"

George had been hit hard a few times before. Ronnie Ryan's fist had hit George's jaw on numerous occasions. Sometimes George could joke his way out of a hiding and sometimes he couldn't. Today, as he hit the deck as Tommy's punch landed on his chin, he knew it was one of those times he couldn't.

"Get up," said Tommy menacingly.

Realising that Tommy wanted to hit him again, George, remembering, among other things his own height was barely 1.5 metres, replied, "You're joking, right?"

"Get up," said Tommy menacingly. "Maybe you need a boxing lesson. Maybe you're not so smart after all." Tommy's face was blue with rage. He was nearly crying as he shouted at George on the ground.

Of course, news of Tommy's outburst travelled far around the school.

George didn't speak to Tommy the next day at

English. In fact, Sally Anne had sat behind Tommy at tutorial that morning after giving him a dirty look. I bet they've had a good bitch about me, thought Tommy. He was ashamed of hitting George but most of all, he was ashamed at not having the courage to talk to Sally Anne.

It was Tommy, then, who broke the silence near the end of the English lesson.

"Well, did she meet your kissing standards?" asked Tommy sarcastically.

"What . . . eh? Say again," replied George vaguely.

Tommy saw the bruise on George's chin and felt sorry that he'd hit him the previous day. "George, I don't know what came over me yester-day."

"What are you talking about Tommy?"

"When I hit you –"

"Oh that," said George, as if he'd been think-ing of something else. "Think nothing of it Tommy. I don't mean to be cheeky but I know I must sound it sometimes."

"I thought you weren't speaking to me because of our punch-up yesterday," said Tommy.

There was a long pause until George whispered, "It's not that. I kissed Sally Anne."

"Oh!" said Tommy loudly enough for Mrs Gray to hear.

"No talking, Tommy," she said "It's bad enough that you didn't do your homework last night and were fighting in the playground, but do you have to keep George off his work too? Really, What's wrong with you lately? Back to work."

"I won't be kissing her again," said George quietly.

"Why not?" asked Tommy.

"Have you heard of that spider in South America. You know, the female that paralyses the male with a bite, then kills him?" For once George's joking tone appeared to have deserted him.

"Eh, I'm not sure."

"Well, I was walking her back to class after lunch. We'd just shared my corned beef . . ."

"Oh, very classy, how to impress a Champagne Lady . . ." laughed Tommy.

". . . sandwiches when I deemed the moment to be right for kissing."

"All those years of experience, eh, and you're only thirteen as well. Well, did you deem the wrong moment? Did your scientific methods of deciding the right moment let you down, Mr Borden?"

"No, it was the right moment. But . . ." George broke off.

"But what?" asked Tommy now very interested.

"Well, it's spooky really."

"Don't tell me you were scared – champion kisser."

George paused then said, "I – I was."

The bell rang for the end of the lesson. As they filed out Tommy said to George, "Let's nip round to the shops."

"You mean skip the next lesson?"

"Yeah, I want to hear about this. I'm a little spooked out myself about this girl," said Tommy.

They sat on a wall outside the newsagents eating their ice lollies. Both George and Tommy knew that they'd be missed from art class and that they'd have some tricky explaining to do.

"So, George, tell me about this kiss."

Again George hesitated. "Well, I kinda –," he searched for the right word, "froze, I suppose."

"Froze, I suppose," repeated Tommy. "Taken up poetry have you."

"It's not funny, Tommy. I reached out and held her. She seemed to think it was a good idea. And I kissed her. But her lips felt so cold."

"In the middle of summer?"

"Exactly, but that was just the start of it. Her lips weren't cold, they were freezing. My mind went blank. I couldn't move. I couldn't think. Not only had my own lips become cold, but the air felt cold and I remember thinking, this is what it must feel like if you kiss a ghost."

"A ghost," gasped Tommy.

"Yeah, a ghost. I mean, I don't believe in all that stuff but it was freaky."

"Are you sure you weren't imagining all this?" asked Tommy sarcastically.

"I though so at first because in my mind I started to see all sorts of things from another time."

"What do you mean?" inquired Tommy.

"No, it's too weird, you won't believe me."

Tommy sat halfheartedly eating his ice lolly, distracted by the crazy talk from George. He was wondering whether or not to let George in on his little secret. A secret that he barely understood himself but, since George had been talking it all made strange sense.

"I do believe you," said Tommy, breaking the awkward silence.

"You do? If you'd told me this bizarre story, I don't think I'd have believed you."

Here goes, thought Tommy as he prepared to tell George his secret.

"Do you promise not to tell anyone *my* weird dream?" asked Tommy.

"Okay."

"Well, the day before Sally Anne started in our

class, I had a dream about a beautiful girl and when I first saw Sally Anne, she reminded me so much of this beautiful girl. I thought she was the same girl but that couldn't be . . . could it?"

"Go on," encouraged George.

"In the dream she said, 'I'm coming for you. We have unfinished business. You have to let me help you.' But whenever I asked her what it was she had to help me with she just looked frightened and said, 'Don't you remember?'"

"In the dream she was familiar to me but I couldn't remember where I'd seen her before. In fact she was offended by this. I woke up saying 'Tell me.'"

"I thought no more of it. Even when I saw her the next day, supposedly for the first time, I decided that it was just a coincidence that she looked like the girl in my dream."

"A – a dream?" George interrupted. "That's what it was like when I kissed her. Like I was taken in a dream."

At that moment, they both stopped talking.

They saw Sally Anne walking up the hill towards the newsagents.

As she approached, she smiled at them. Worried and confused, the boys smiled back unconvincingly.

"Mr Bush is asking where you are," she said, "both of you."

Chapter 4

Mr Bush was called "Mr Brush" by the pupils because it sounded more fitting for an art teacher. He also lost his temper a lot so the children sometimes called him "Old Burning", as in burning bush. He was only forty-two but to the children anything over sixteen years of age was "getting on a bit" so forty-two years old was definitely old. So Old Burning Bush was old and scary. So when George and Tommy walked into the class with only ten minutes of the lesson remaining, Old Burning let off a fair bit of steam at them.

"I'm responsible for you while you're meant

to be in my class. If anything happened to you I'd get into big trouble," he shouted.

"It's nice of you to show such concern for us, Old Burn . . . I mean, Mr Bush," said George.

Mr Bush told them to take their seats and just do nothing for the last few remaining minutes of the lesson.

"George," whispered Tommy.

"What?"

"Look at Sally Anne's painting."

Some pupils in the art class had obviously been painting a bunch of flowers.

"I hope you've enjoyed your lesson in still life," Mr Bush remarked.

"It doesn't look still alive to me," shouted Ronnie Ryan, to much laughter.

"Keep your mouth shut, Ryan, if you want to stay alive," growled old Bush.

"I'd stay alive all right, Mr Bush. After all, you've explained how you're responsible for my welfare while I'm in your class," said Ronnie, with the air of a smart Alec.

"Exactly – while you're in my class. I didn't say anything about what could happen to you outside my class, did I?" replied Mr Bush, threateningly.

Ronnie shut up.

Once this minor commotion died down, George did what Tommy had previously asked and looked at Sally Anne's painting. It looked great. Why had Tommy asked him to look at it though, thought George. Neither of them cared for art much.

"So?" enquired George outside the art class as pupils fought to get out in the fresh air of the playground.

"So?" replied Tommy. "Does nothing strike you as odd about the painting?"

George though about it before replying. "Well, she's painted a village instead of those scabby begonias and I'd have used a lighter shade of grey for the sky," he said sarcastically, then added, "What do I know about paintings? What was odd about it?"

"It was finished, wasn't it?"

"Yes, so what?"

"In fact, George, Sally Anne's painting was the only one that was finished in class."

"Get to the point, Tommy."

"Well, how could she have had time to finish it? After all, didn't she come round to the shops to tell us that Mr Bush was waiting for us?"

"Yeah, but she got back before us remember? She ran on ahead of us back to the class," reasoned George.

"But the school is a good ten minute walk from the shop – and ten minutes back again."

"What are you getting at Tommy?"

"And she stood talking to us – or should I say, you – for about five minutes."

"And still managed to get back to class and finish that painting?" asked George.

"Exactly – there wasn't enough time."

"Unless she happens to be a gifted artist," said George, cautiously.

"She'd need to be better and quicker than anyone else. I mean, Lucy Stevenson is the best by far – agreed?" asked Tommy.

"Yeah . . ."

"Well, even she didn't finish on time."

"So, Sally Anne's good at art – big deal," said George, losing interest in this chain of thought. "See you tomorrow," he said as he ran to catch the school bus home.

Tommy walked home slowly, with a puzzled expression on his face. He heard footsteps behind him, as he looked behind he was surprised to see Sally Anne catching him up.

"Hi, Tommy," she said.

Chapter 5

"I hope Mr Bush didn't scare you too much," she said, mockingly.

"I can see why you and George get on so well – you both think you have a sense of humour," said Tommy.

"Oh, and what else do you imagine we have in common?" she asked, sensing Tommy was a little put out.

"Neither of you are funny," said Tommy as he continued walking.

"There's no need to be rude, Tommy."

"I didn't think you were talking to me anyway. I thought you were siding with your kissing partner after I hit him."

"I know," she said thinking.

"Well, this is me here," said Tommy at his gate.

"Aren't you going to invite me in for coffee," she said laughing.

Tommy was gob-smacked. "Why?" he said curiously.

"Because we have a lot to talk about."

Tommy couldn't remember inviting her in exactly but there he was, pouring milk into her coffee and nervously offering her biscuits.

But, he felt very comfortable with her. He couldn't explain it.

Then she came right out with it.

"Tommy, keep this to yourself, all right – but I'm a witch."

Tommy stared at her from his seat as she calmly sipped her coffee.

"Lovely coffee, Tommy – what is it, Brazilian?"

Tommy just stared.

"Don't say you hadn't guessed," she said.

Tommy then started to giggle. He caught himself quickly but still had terrible trouble stopping.

"Don't laugh in her face," he thought, "she might actually *believe* that she is a witch. After all, George thinks he's a comedian, Mr Bush thinks he's an art teacher – she thinks she's a witch – hey, it's a mixed-up, screwed-up crazy world, ain't it?"

She continued sipping her coffee in silence. Tommy was still letting out the odd snigger.

"These chocolate biscuits are good, aren't they?" she said. "That's a hint that I'd like another one," she added.

Tommy grabbed a couple and passed the biscuit tin to her across the table, saying, "Only if you promise not to read my palm," he laughed at his own joke.

She just took the biscuits and smiled, then she said, "I don't need to read your palm."

"Go on then fortune teller, what does my future hold?"

"You're obsessed by the future. You're always thinking about passing exams, going to university, getting a job as a reporter. In a way, you're already living in the future. You can probably guess your own future without help from the likes of me," said Sally Anne.

"So, I shouldn't think so much about the future. Is that what you're saying?"

"I didn't say that. George would say that, wouldn't he?" said Sally Anne.

"Oh yes, your mate George, whom you've known for all of one week," said Tommy raising his eyes.

"But I'm right. He always says, live for now — am I right?" she asked earnestly.

"Okay, so you're right. So what. So I'm for the future, George is for the present and you're for . . . what . . . which one are you for?"

"Which one have you missed out?" asked Sally Anne mischievously.

"Dunno, you tell me oh, soothsayer," Tommy was barely interested.

"The past," she said.

"What do you mean?" asked Tommy.

"The future is important," she said. "But George is right in a way, too. You have to live for the present too, it's also important."

"You sound more like an agony aunt than a witch."

"But the past," she continued, ignoring Tommy's mocking, "is important too."

"You mean childhood and all that – what are you, some kind of high school psychiatrist?"

"I'm a witch remember – I'm talking about past lives – not earlier in this life," said Sally Anne.

At this Tommy just burst out laughing and he couldn't stop.

"I'm sorry, I'm sorry," he repeated between giggles and full blown belly laughs.

Once Tommy's laughter had died down, Sally Anne reminded him about her painting in Mr Bush's art class.

"I'm a good painter, Tommy, aren't I?" she teased.

"But that doesn't make you a witch."

"Why, I must be the quickest artist in the class, eh, perhaps in the world."

Tommy paused, the laughter was replaced now by silence. Eventually he said "Okay, I admit that seemed spooky."

"And George's story about him kissing me, didn't that make both of you think?" she said.

"How did you know about him telling me that?"

"I was in the art class yesterday and wondered where both of you were. Then I sensed you were talking about me. True, I want you to know the truth about me – but no-one else. So I interrupted your little chat at the shops. Mr Bush didn't even notice you weren't in class. I made that up to get you back to class and to stop talking about me. I was worried George might guess something near the truth."

"The truth?" asked Tommy. "I don't think there was much danger of either of us guessing that you were a witch."

"Maybe not," said Sally Anne. "But he did say that kissing me was like kissing a ghost, didn't he?"

"You weren't there when he said that. How did you know that?"

Tommy looked alarmed. First she had said she sensed he and George had been at the shops. Okay, she could have stumbled upon them quite by chance. She'd said she sensed them talking about her – okay, she'd kissed George the day before, so that was an educated guess on her part. But now she'd reminded Tommy that George had likened kissing her to kissing a ghost. That was pretty precise.

Sally Anne sat quietly. She emptied the last drops of coffee from the cup.

"So which are you – a witch or a ghost?" asked Tommy challengingly.

"We're all ghosts, Tommy. We've all lived before. We're back here again to get things right that we got wrong the last time."

"Isn't that what Buddhists believe?"

"It isn't just a Buddhist belief. But it doesn't matter what people believe," said Sally Anne.

Tommy's mother was walking up the path to the back door. He could see her through the big window in the kitchen struggling with various bags of shopping.

"What do you believe, Tommy?"

"I believe in the future – not the past," said Tommy, getting up to go and help his mother with the shopping. He looked back at Sally Anne as she was putting her school blazer on. He smiled at her.

She said "One day, Tommy, you'll see that much of what you call your present life is just an illusion. Who's to say what is real?"

Tommy was walking out the back door as she said this. He was anxious to introduce Sally Anne to his mother, providing she kept her witchy talk to herself.

"Hi Mum," he said, talking some of the bags from her. "Here, let me help. By the way, I'd like to introduce you to a new classmate of mine. She likes your taste in coffee." Tommy was talking excitedly. Although Sally Anne wasn't his girlfriend, he felt sure she would be one day.

"She?" asked Mrs McDonald teasingly.

"No wisecracks, Mum, she's just a friend," he whispered as they walked into the kitchen.

But the kitchen table was empty.

"Well," said his mother.

"She was sitting right here," said Tommy. "Maybe she got nervous about meeting you and left," said Tommy, very annoyed at Sally Anne's rudeness, even if it was down to nerves.

"Don't worry about it, son," she said. She started clearing away the coffee cup and saucer on the table and said "I thought you liked that Brazilian coffee."

"I do," replied Tommy.

"Well, why didn't you have a cup then?" his mother asked.

"I did," said Tommy, puzzled.

"Well, why is there just one cup and saucer used? Did you and your girlfriend – sorry, classmate – share the same cup?" inquired Mrs McDonald.

"No, of course not."

"Well, if you had a cup and she had a cup, why is there only one cup?" Mrs McDonald paused, looked at Tommy and said "You don't need to make up stories, Tommy. You'll get round to bringing girls home soon enough. You don't need to try to impress the world by telling fibs. There was no girl here, was there, son?"

Tommy was flabbergasted.

"What? Why do you think I'd make up something like that? If I was to make up impressive stories, I'd tell you I'd robbed a bank, or had been to the moon. But, having a cup of coffee with a classmate . . . you've got to believe me, she was right there." Then he remembered that she'd eaten a few of the chocolate biscuits. "Here, look at this," he said, opening the biscuit tin. To his amazement, the packet of biscuits was unopened.

"What is it, Tommy?" asked his mother.

"Nothing," said Tommy, staring at the full packet of biscuits. "I think maybe I fell asleep and had a dream."

But of course he knew it was *not* a dream.

Chapter 6

Sally Anne sat beside Tommy the next morning at tutorial.

"Okay," said Tommy. "I'm not sure if you're a witch, a ghost or just a practical joker."

"What do you mean?" asked Sally Anne, feigning innocence.

"You win, I'm interested to hear more of your story and why you're here."

"What are you talking about, Tommy?" she asked impatiently.

"Yesterday – the case of the disappearing coffee cup, the witch conversation, your vanishing act

– what do you think I'm talking about?" said Tommy, confused.

"Yesterday?"

"Yes, yesterday!"

"But you don't believe in the past, do you Tommy? Perhaps I was never in your house."

"Okay, I know something strange is going on. You've made your point, now can you tell me what your game is?"

"All right, Tommy," said Sally Anne. "After school, why don't you come back to my house and I'll explain everything."

"Should I be frightened?" asked Tommy, smirking slightly.

"Yes!"

Tommy stopped smirking.

Chapter 7

In the playground at lunchtime, George saw Tommy walking about as if his head was in the clouds.

"Oi, dreamy," he shouted at Tommy, "stop pretending something interesting is going on inside that empty head of yours."

"Hi, George."

"Tommy, I was thinking about what you said about Sally Anne's painting. It is spooky, isn't it?" said George.

By now Tommy wanted to be the only one to know Sally Anne's secret. So he pretended to

George that he'd solved the mystery of the fastest painter in school history.

"Well, I spoke to Sally Anne last night."

"Last night? You mean you met her out of school?" asked George, surprised.

"What's the big deal? She said she had done that same painting lots of times and that's what made it easy for her to do it quickly," lied Tommy.

"So, no mystery then?" asked George, sounding a little unconvinced.

"None."

"Well, perhaps you're right, Tommy," George looked as if he was thinking.

"Now it's you who's pretending to have something interesting going on inside your head," commented Tommy.

"Did you look closely at that picture, Tommy?" asked George mysteriously.

"Not all that closely, why?" asked Tommy, puzzled.

"Because you're in it!" said George.

George took Tommy to the art class straight

away. Mr Bush was doing some paperwork at his desk. George knocked on the door.

"Come in," said Mr Bush, adding "if you must."

"Hello, sir, do you mind if we look at some of the paintings you've put on the wall this week?" asked George.

Mr Bush regularly put recent paintings by pupils up on his wall. Not because he was interested, or appreciated his talented pupils, but to show Mrs Lewis, the Head of the Art Department, that his pupils actually did something. No doubt, he believed that this was because he was a wonderful teacher. Mrs Lewis was once heard telling him that it was in spite of his teaching skills that his pupils achieved anything. Because he wasn't interested in his pupils' work, he hadn't looked at Sally Anne's picture very closely when he put it on the wall the day before.

"So, you've become an art critic?" said Mr Bush suspiciously.

"No, not at all, sir. Just looking for ways to improve my own work," said George.

"And you need young Mr McDonald to help you, do you?" asked Mr Bush.

"No," said Tommy, "I want to improve my work too."

Mr Bush looked piercingly at both of the boys. He remembered Mrs Lewis saying that she was disappointed that he didn't encourage his pupils to take an interest in art. With this in mind, he said: "Okay, but don't make any noise, and don't be long."

Tommy looked at the painting. It was of an old village. It looked like a scene from a Charles Dickens book. There was a grubby factory in the background and a boy and a girl on a cart being driven by a very old looking horse. The cart seemed to be carrying coal. It was quite a bleak painting, cloudy sky, dark colours and unsmiling people.

"Look at the boy on the cart," said George. He was the absolute double of Tommy. But Tommy was looking at the girl on the cart. She was the double of Sally Anne. The boy and the girl were the only people smiling in the picture.

"That place looks so familiar," said Tommy.

"She must have a crush on you, Tommy," said George.

"Shhhhh!" said Mr Bush.

"Come on, George," said Tommy, "let's go get something to eat."

Chapter 8

"Aren't you going to eat your chips?" asked George.

That was the first piece of conversation between George and Tommy since they had looked at the picture. Tommy sat, deep in thought, at their table in the dinner hall.

"That picture was so familiar," said Tommy at last.

"Of course it was, you saw it in the art class the other day," said George.

"No, I don't mean the picture," said Tommy. "I mean the whole scene. I feel like I've been there before. The factory, the village – they looked so familiar."

"Maybe you've seen it in a book or something, or . . ."

"That's it – in the dream!"

"What dream?" asked George.

"The dream I had the night before Sally Anne turned up in our class."

"Oh, that dream," said George.

"Of course," replied Tommy. "It's too weird. I still can't make sense of it. I can't remember the dream very well, but the minute I saw Sally Anne, I was sure I recognised her. And now that picture . . . maybe we *have* lived before."

"Lived before? What do you mean?"

"Nothing, oh, who knows? I'll ask her tonight."

"Tonight?" George was now exasperated. "What do you mean, tonight? In fact, never mind that, what do you mean 'lived before'? You know, Tommy, maybe there is something interesting going on in your head after all!"

"I'll tell you about it tomorrow – if it makes any sense, that is," said Tommy.

Tommy was quiet for the rest of the day. He barely heard George saying "See you tomorrow", as he got the school bus home that evening. Tommy was too intrigued by Sally Anne, living before, the picture, witches, ghosts and lots of other stuff.

In the meantime, what Tommy did not know was that George was sitting on the top deck of the school feeling very distracted. Why? Because when he kissed Sally Anne the other day, in addition to feeling like he was kissing a ghost, he felt like he was being transported back in time. In fact, he seemed to fall into a hypnotic trance and he vividly remembered the village, the factory, the tired old horse, the girl on the cart. In other words, when George kissed Sally Anne, he seemed to be transported back in time, into the scene that Sally Anne painted in class. George had thought it had been his imagination but, after having seen the painting, he was now totally spooked. But, when he was in his trance, he did not see anyone sitting beside the Sally Anne lookalike on the cart in the picture. George remembered her, unsmiling and on her own. Apart from that one detail, the picture was pretty much a replica of the scene he remembered from his trance.

Of course, George – good old happy-go-lucky George – would not be the kind of lad to talk deeply of trances and so on. But he felt something was going on. Even Tommy – super sensible Tommy McDonald – thought the picture was familiar. But, wondered George, where did Tommy recognise the picture from; just from his dream? There seemed to be more to it than that. George decided to act as if he wasn't all that interested in the whole affair. Nevertheless, he was secretly fascinated by the whole thing and could hardly wait to hear what Tommy had to say tomorrow.

Chapter 9

Sally Anne crept up behind Tommy at the school gates and suddenly shouted, "Gotcha!"

"For goodness sake," screeched Tommy. Then he realised that it was only Sally Anne larking around.

"You're still not funny," he said sourly.

"Oh, cheer up, you young fuddy duddy. Come on, we'll miss the train," she said, walking ahead quickly.

"Train?" shouted Tommy after her.

"Yeah. I don't live in this part of town. Come on," she called back to Tommy.

If she didn't live in this part of town, thought Tommy, why did she go to this school?

They just made it to the train on time. Sally Anne flashed her weekly student's train pass to the Inspector, who looked too bored to check it properly.

"You said earlier that I should be frightened," said Tommy, not quite convinced that he should be.

"Well," she said, "that depends on how open minded you are."

"What do you mean?" asked Tommy.

"I don't know if you're ready for this or not, but here goes. Watch this."

Sally Anne stood up in the train compartment and walked to the carriage door.

"Excuse me, everybody. Listen up people," she shouted. "Everybody, listen to me, please."

Tommy was so embarrassed he crouched down in his seat as far as he could. Sally Anne continued.

"I'd like to sing you all a song." And she burst into "She loves you, yeah, yeah, yeah," an old

Beatles song. She was dancing! Then she stood on a spare seat next to a very respectable, boring, middle aged man. She was clapping her hands, singing at the top of her voice.

Tommy was agog. He now closed his eyes and pretended to be asleep. Sally Anne saw him do so and decided to draw attention to him.

"Listen up once again, folks. I've got some scandal for you. See yonder, on that seat over there," Tommy knew she was pointing to his seat. "Over there sits Tommy McDonald. Never kissed a girl, not one."

Shut up, for goodness sake, shut up. Tommy said mentally, wondering what on earth had got into Sally Anne.

He nervously looked up, expecting to see the whole compartment full of people staring at him. To his amazement, everything was as before. No-one had stirred. In fact, they were all still doing what they had been doing before Sally Anne started her palaver. In fact, it looked like Sally Anne was invisible to them! He stood up and said, "Sally

Anne . . ." but, before he could continue, just about everyone in the compartment looked around to see why he was standing up calling out a girl's name!

"They can't see or hear me," shouted Sally Anne.

"But they can hear me," said Tommy without thinking. And, of course, the other passengers looked at him once more, wondering if he was a mad man.

"Yes, they can hear you all right. But not me. Watch this," said Sally Anne mischievously. She went right up to an old man without hair and said, "Hello Baldy, where's your hair?"

Again, Tommy didn't think before he spoke and blurted out, "Sally Anne! Really! It's not his fault he's got no hair!"

The old man with no hair looked up at Tommy. "Are you talking about me, sonny?"

"No, no, of course not," said Tommy.

Another bald man further down the carriage stood up and said angrily, "Well, in that case, the cheeky young rascal must be talking about me."

"No, no, honestly, it was a mistake. I'm sorry." Tommy was really confused now.

"Well then," said another man, taking his hat off, revealing his own bald head, "he must be talking about me."

It was like a nightmare. All three of the bald men got up from their seats and started walking slowly towards Tommy.

"You need a lesson in manners, you cheeky young fellow," said one of them.

"Honestly, no, it was a mistake. I wasn't talking about any of you," he pleaded, stepping away from the advancing men.

"In that case," said the voice of a fourth man who had hair, "you must be talking about me!" And he put his hands up to his head and pulled at his hair. It was a wig! He too, was bald after all!

"How did you know it was a wig, young man? Are you a spy?" asked the fourth man.

This is going from bad to worse thought Tommy.

"How would I know you were bald? What do you mean, a spy? Sally Anne?" he cried out.

Suddenly, the train stopped. It was nowhere near a station. Suddenly, all the passengers were seated again. The man with the wig had his wig back on. The bald man with the hat had his hat back on. Both were reading newspapers as if nothing had happened. Tommy sat down quickly and wondered was it all a dream, a trance.

The train started moving again. Sally Anne appeared sitting beside Tommy. All that could be heard now was the noise of the train shuddering along the line.

"Did that really happen?" said Tommy to Sally Anne.

"Yes," said Sally Anne.

"But . . ." Tommy looked at everyone sitting as if nothing had happened. "Why are they . . ."

"They don't remember," interrupted Sally Anne.

"They don't remember?" said Tommy incredulously.

"They don't remember," repeated Sally Anne.

"How come?" asked Tommy.

"I've hypnotised them. Are you any closer to believing me – that I'm a witch?"

"I'm closer to going out of my mind," said Tommy, completely at a loss. "How do I know," added Tommy, "that you didn't hypnotise me, and none of that happened?"

"Fair question. You'll just have to trust me."

The train pulled into the station on a side of town that Tommy didn't recognise.

"Where's this then?" asked Tommy, trying to come out of the daze brought on by the spooky incident on the train.

"We're in my home village," said Sally Anne.

"I've never been here before," said Tommy.

She looked at him closely and smiled. "Are you sure nothing strikes you as familiar?" she asked.

Tommy looked around and looked for something to recognise. He vaguely recognised the general outlay of the main street, but then again all small villages tended to look a little alike.

"No, I don't think so," he said.

"Well, you should do – this is where you were born," said Sally Anne.

"But I was born in Belldale. That's hundreds of miles from here," he said.

"Maybe in this life, but in your previous life, you were born here."

"I don't believe in all that stuff – too far-fetched."

"Oh, really, well I can think of a lot of far-fetched things that you believe."

"What like?"

"You believe in the future. You believe you're going to be a journalist, pass your exams and lots of other things," she said.

"So, I know where I'm going. So do lots of people," said Tommy. "What's wrong with that?"

"I didn't say there's anything wrong with it, but if you believe in the future why not the past? Do you want more proof?"

Tommy thought about her disappearing act at his house – and the train journey. But, even although these things spooked him, he wasn't certain that Sally Anne was a witch. She might just be a mixed up girl with nothing better to do. But why had she taken up with him? "Why me?" he thought.

"Okay then, if you're offering more proof, then fire away – do your worst," he challenged, although he was a little apprehensive.

Sally Anne looked disappointed and then, after thinking for a few moments, said, "Okay, watch this."

Sally Anne reached out her hands to Tommy's face and held it for a moment, then kissed him.

Tommy didn't have time to react and, before he knew it, his mind was whirling. Sally Anne stepped back and Tommy opened his eyes but he was stunned to find himself in a very different setting. He couldn't believe his eyes. He was in the same place, there were signs on shop windows saying Rolwell Bakery and so on, but everybody in the street was dressed in old fashioned clothes – very old fashioned clothes. Victorian, in fact. He was then hit by very strange smells. Then he realised that there were no cars, only horse-drawn carriages. Then he noticed that the road wasn't surfaced with tar, it was just dust, like in an old Wild West movie. The noises were of horses, carts moving, drivers cracking their whips. It was like he had been thrown back in time! Then he looked at Sally Anne, and saw her dressed in the same old fashioned dress that he remembered from the painting she'd done in Mr Bush's art class. He felt dizzy. His mind was trying to make sense of what was going on.

"Wake up," he said aloud to himself. "Wake up, Tommy!"

"You are awake, Tommy. More awake than you normally are. What you call waking hours isn't as awake as this. This is real Tommy – real," said Sally Anne.

He looked around and immediately recognised the old factory from the painting. In fact, everything was exactly the same as in the painting. Suddenly Tommy noticed his clothes felt different and he looked down and realised that he was dressed exactly as the boy in Sally Anne's painting. The same flat cap on his head, the same brown breeches with braces, the same white striped collarless shirt.

"This can't be real! It can't be! It can't be!"

Tommy felt like he was falling asleep. "It can't be, can't be, can't be . . . can't . . ."

Chapter 10

"Wake up, Tommy, wake up," Mrs McDonald was shaking her son.

"It can't be," Tommy was still muttering to himself.

"Wake up, Tommy," said his mother again.

Tommy opened his eyes but found it hard to wake up.

"Where am I?" he mumbled, utterly confused.

"You're in bed, where do you think you are? Hurry up and get up! You'll be late. Come on, Tommy, this is not like you. What's going on in your head these days?" asked Mrs McDonald.

"I wish I knew," said Tommy.

"What?"

"Nothing," he replied drowsily.

Could it be, thought Tommy that Sally Anne, the girl who sat beside him in school, really was a witch? How did he get to bed last night? More to the point, how did he get home? Was it all a dream? After all, he'd dreamt about Sally Anne before.

As he was getting dressed, thinking about all the recent strangeness, he heard his mother shouting to his father.

"David, is this your cap?"

"Cap? I don't have a cap. Do you think I'm an old man or something?"

"Or something," shouted Tommy downstairs.

"Very funny," shouted Dad. "Is this yours, Tommy?"

"Of course it isn't," he heard his mum say sharply to his dad.

Then it struck Tommy. Of course it was his cap! He remembered wearing it when he was mysteriously taken back in time. But how could he be sure?

"Yeah, it is mine actually," said Tommy, grabbing the cap from the breakfast table. He ran out the door, whilst saying, "I'm going to be late" and disappeared out into the street.

Obviously, thought Tommy, my parents haven't asked any questions about yesterday. I must have got home on time and without any suspicious circumstances. Otherwise, they'd be asking awkward questions.

Sally Anne was absent the next day.

"Damn," thought Tommy. "I sure wanted to ask her some questions." He waited until he was in art class later that day before he looked at Sally Anne's painting. He wanted to check the cap on the boy in the cart was wearing to see if it was the same one as was found in his house that morning. That way he'd know for certain if there really was some connection between the picture and his experiences the previous day. Where was Sally Anne? He really wanted to ask her what the hell was going on. And what the hell does she want with me he thought, yet again.

He was first to the art class. He'd given George the slip as the class made their way from the maths room to the art room. He wanted to look quickly at the picture on his own. Tommy glanced around to make sure no-one was paying any attention to him and then opened his school bag. He took out the cap and held it up beside the painting. But the painting was different! It depicted a completely different scene than it had the day before.

Tommy couldn't believe his eyes. I must be looking at the wrong picture he thought – but no – it was signed by Sally Anne. She must have sneaked in and replaced the original, thought Tommy to himself. Somehow, he knew deep down that wasn't true. But it helped calm him for the moment. The new scene showed the same boy and girl, but they were both on a chariot! Like in the Bronze Age. In fact, the people walking beside the chariot looked like Vikings or Saxons maybe. There were no real buildings, only what looked like straw huts.

Tommy wondered whether maybe he should go and see the school nurse and confess that he had lost his marbles! She must have changed the picture. She must have! It was the only explanation. The picture couldn't have changed itself – could it? Tommy didn't know what to believe any more.

He sat down, more befuddled than ever. George sat down beside him.

"Have I done anything wrong?" asked George.

"No, why?"

"Because I don't think you've said two words to me all day. What's the matter – too busy thinking about your future again?" teased George.

"Worrying about my past, more like," replied Tommy.

"What are you talking about now?" laughed George.

"George, go and have a look at Sally Anne's picture after class."

"Why?"

"Just have a look."

"Okay, okay."

Chapter 11

At the end of the class, most of the pupils filed out quickly. Mr Bush saw George and Tommy looking at Sally Anne's picture.

"What is it that fascinates you about that picture?" he asked gruffly.

"Did Sally Anne paint this picture recently, sir?" asked George.

"Are you being cheeky, son? You were here when she did it, weren't you?"

"But that's not the same one," said Tommy, pointing to the new one on the wall.

"Of course it is," said Mr Bush.

"You mean no-one's changed them over?"

Tommy was interrupted by Mr Bush. "Get away with you. Go on, go to your next class, you pair of chatter boxes. Of course no-one's changed them over. What kind of prank would that be? Shouldn't you be away squeezing your spots or worrying about BO or whatever you kids are meant to do? Cheeky devils," shouted Mr Bush as he ushered them out of his classroom. "Hurry back, only next time bring your brains, please."

And with that Mr Bush slammed the door.

"Cheeky old git," said George.

"Perhaps we could get Sally Anne to place a spell on him," said Tommy, laughing for the first time that day.

"As if she's a witch," laughed George, not knowing how true it might be. "Prettiest witch I ever saw," he added, smiling.

"Really, well how come you stopped chasing her after your first kiss?" asked Tommy slyly.

George went awfully quiet.

Tommy realised that he might get some clues from George by asking him for the full story of what happened between George and Sally Anne. So he asked George for the full facts. George simply told him that he and Sally Anne had a short kiss and that was that. George again mentioned that something spooky happened but he had trouble remembering it all.

"In fact," George said, "I can't remember what really happened, and what was a dream. I'm not sure if I didn't imagine the whole thing. The only thing I remember was her last words that night."

"What were they?" asked Tommy eagerly.

"She just said, 'No, you're not the one, after all.'"

"At least she's honest," said Tommy cruelly.

"No, I mean it was like she was looking for someone in particular."

"Ain't we all, mate!"

"No, but it was as if she could only tell from the kiss."

"You're not making any sense, George," pretended Tommy. But, of course, George was making perfect sense to Tommy.

But really, there was only one person who could make sense of the whole picture. Where, thought Tommy, was Sally Anne?

Chapter 12

"How was school today?" asked Tommy's mum when she came in.

"Fine," said Tommy automatically.

"I meant to ask you this morning, Tommy, where did you get that cap?" asked Mum.

"From the olden days," said Tommy, getting up from the kitchen table to go to his room.

"Very funny," said his mum, a little curious.

Tommy was lying on his bed, scanning his bookshelves. He was trying to distract himself from the growing mystery of the witch, Sally Anne, if she really was a witch.

Just at that moment, he saw a picture of Sally

Anne in his mind. He closed his eyes and saw it more clearly. She was picking up a phone. Am I dreaming? he wondered, trying to snap out of it. Am I imagining this? His head felt strained. He had a vision of Sally Anne dialling numbers on a phone. He tried to see what the numbers were, but he could only make out the last four digits; 4, 1, 8, 1.

"Hey," he thought, "that's the last four digits of my telephone number!"

Just at that exact moment, the vision disappeared and Tommy could hear the phone ringing in the downstairs hall. He heard his father pick it up.

"Hello," said Dad. "Yes, I'll just check . . . Tommy!" he shouted, "That's for you."

Tommy was numb. Wow! Perhaps there is something in this clairvoyancy thing after all. He was trying to make light of it. Anyway, it couldn't be Sally Anne. She didn't even know his number.

"It'll be George," he thought.

As he was walking down the stairs, he heard his mum ask his dad who was on the phone for Tommy.

Tommy's dad replied: "She says it's an old girlfriend."

"An old one!" exclaimed his mother, "Tommy's never had a girlfriend – at least not as far as I know."

Tommy looked at the phone handset lying on the telephone table. Should he pick it up? His mother was right. He'd never had a girlfriend. At least he thought, half joking, at least not in this life. He picked it up.

"Hello."

"Hello, Tommy."

It was Sally Anne!

"That's right, Tommy, not in this life," she said, as if she had just read Tommy's mind.

"We've got to talk," he said impatiently.

"Who's that girl on the phone, Tommy?" shouted his mother, getting up from her chair.

"You got a cutie stashed away that you've not told us about!" shouted his dad, also getting up.

"We'll have to get that phone tapped," laughed Mrs McDonald. "It's the only way we'll find out what's going on around here," she added.

"Tommy," called Sally Anne down the 'phone, trying to get Tommy's attention back. "Meet me at the train station in an hour."

"How did you get my number?" But she'd hung up.

The train station!

"Reasons to be worried –" thought Tommy, "One: she knows my number. Two: it's dark. Three: that last train journey with Sally-Anne drove me mental. Four: it's raining and I'll get wet. Five: Mum and Dad are taking too big an interest in what they think is my love life. Six: I don't have a love life. Seven: I'm panicking."

While counting up the reasons to be worried, he had gone up the stairs, changed into his jeans and denim jacket and at the same time, fended off question after question from his nosy parents.

"Tommy, you're not listening. Where are you going?" said Mum.

"Is something wrong, son?" asked Dad as

Tommy jumped down the last few stairs on the stairway.

"I think there is something wrong, Jean," he heard his dad's now distant voice say to his mother.

"What a detective," thought Tommy sarcastically. "Eight: my parents are thick! Nine: where does that leave me?! Ten: what the heck am I doing out here?"

He was now at the station. He was about half an hour early. He was soaking wet. He was tired, confused. The half hour passed slowly, but it passed.

Eleven: here comes Sally Anne!

Chapter 13

"Okay," said Tommy full of purpose "what's going on? This mystery has to be cleared up tonight."

"It will be," said Sally Anne.

"Okay, start talking," said Tommy.

"You're so difficult to convince, Tommy. You won't believe me if I just tell you. I want to show you once more, what you would call strange things. I think it's the only way I can persuade you of my reason for being here."

"I don't know if I can take any more. The last two days seem to have been a blur. I don't feel as if I've had a moment's sleep. I know I've some explaining to do to my parents – but what can I explain? I don't have a clue," said Tommy, running his hands through his hair.

"Tommy, if only you'd had faith. Then I wouldn't have had to put you through all this."

"I feel so disorientated," said Tommy.

"No, that's not the right word," said Sally-Anne. "All that's really happened to you is that you've had your mind opened . . ."

"You can say that again!" said Tommy.

". . . for the better. How can you understand strange things, special things, if you don't have an open mind?"

"Well then, Doctor Spook," said Tommy, his voice sounding bitter, "is my mind open enough yet?"

"Almost."

Tommy sighed and then said: "What if I just say goodbye and not give all this stuff a second thought? What if I told you to leave me alone? All this would be forgotten, wouldn't it? And if that's the case, then it's not important is it. I don't have to go through this. I don't care any more whether you're a witch or what. I just want to go back to my real life. The one I was certain about before you came on the scene."

"You can run but you can't hide. I've chased you through the centuries, not because I want to – because I have to!"

"Chased me through the centuries!" exclaimed Tommy. "This just gets worse." He paused. "I'm trying to believe you. I want this solved! But I can't. I just can't accept all this stuff."

"That's why we are going on one last train to Rolwell. I knew you wouldn't believe me. This time, if you really want to solve this puzzle, you'll have to do what I say."

"And if I don't . . ."

"And if you don't, I'll leave you alone for the rest of this life. And you'll be a journalist. A successful one. You'll have everything you want, within reason. But in your old age, you'll wonder about this episode. It will prey on your mind. It will become more important to you as you realise that you only have a few years left. You will feel frustration that you didn't check it out. That frustration will sour your last years. You'll realise, as most people do when they are running out of time, that one of the purposes of your life was to face all questions, with or without fear. All your journalistic triumphs will appear valueless beside your regrets. Because, no matter what you achieve, you'll believe you could have achieved more. And if only you'd faced this episode with courage, perhaps you'd have found a great secret. When you wonder what life was all about, you'll wish you had explored every mystery thoroughly."

Tommy was listening. He knew how to plan his future, but he knew what Sally Anne was saying was true. He could visualise himself an old man, sitting in a comfortable chair, on a freshly cut lawn, in some beautiful sun-drenched Mediterranean garden, pondering on his life. He knew it would niggle him that he never followed up on what a journalist would call a great story. He knew also that somehow he'd missed a chance to explore the potential of past lives, clairvoyance, ghosts – everything that the world had wanted for centuries to know more about.

Sally Anne stood staring at him, waiting for Tommy to agree to come on the train. The rain was still teeming down on them. They were on the platform and the noise of the train coming into the station interrupted Tommy's thoughts. He knew now that he had to face whatever mystery lay behind all this.

"Should I be scared?" he asked again, knowing the answer. But he was resigned to going on the train anyway.

"That depends on how open your mind is," said Sally Anne, faintly smiling.

Tommy reached out and opened the train door for Sally Anne. She boarded and looked round for Tommy. He was still on the platform. He seemed to be gathering up all his courage before he followed her. The train started moving. He jumped on.

They found seats and sat down.

"Why Rolwell?" asked Tommy. "What's the significance of Rolwell?"

"Like I said," replied Sally Anne, "It's your home town. I can show you around and I know it will gradually become more familiar to you the more we talk.

"Do you mean I really have lived before?"

"Yes. Lots of times."

"You too?" he asked.

"Of course. Everybody on this train has. Everybody in the world has."

"What for?" asked Tommy.

"Steady on Tommy. I may be a witch, a white witch I stress, but that doesn't mean I can solve the riddle of what life is all about," she laughed.

"But you know more about it than me," said Tommy, who was hoping for more enlightenment than Sally Anne was so far offering.

"Well, I can make you aware of the rights and wrongs of our past lives. I can point out what changes you wanted to make in your last life. I don't know it all, but I know that we live again in order to have second chance to succeed at the things we failed at last time. We all have to move on but, if we're stuck at the same bit, every lifetime, we need help to overcome whatever it is that's holding us back."

"This is heavy. I can't pretend to understand all you're telling me," said Tommy, puzzled.

Sally Anne thought for a moment then said: "Watch this. See that guy sitting there beside the window?" she asked, pointing across to the other side of the carriage.

"Yeah . . ." replied Tommy suspiciously.

"I can show you a short history of him. I can show you what he looked like in his past lives."

Tommy was not about to challenge her after all he'd been through, but he was curious to see this.

"Okay," he said. "This will be an original way to pass a train journey!" Tommy was trying to sound sceptical, but Sally Anne knew he wasn't really sceptical any more. Still, it couldn't do any harm.

"First," she said, "you have to kiss me."

"What?!"

"Tommy, you and I are linked by a love that is very, very old. The power of it has built up over many centuries. This power is unique and special. It is this force that enables me to show you all these strange things. That is why you've got to kiss me."

Tommy thought about it. He always was analytical. He thought Sally Anne's statement sounded logical. He also noticed that he wasn't really scared any more. Just curious, very curious. So, for that reason, he leaned over the table between them and said: "Come here, then."

Sally Anne moved forward and they kissed. Instantly, Tommy fell back into his seat. He could see stars. The colours of everything in the carriage were changing by the second. The man that Sally Anne had pointed to earlier seemed to glow. Slightly at first, then gradually, his dull, drab brown overcoat seemed to be a bright yellow light surrounding him. The man continued to stare out the train window, unaware of anything strange occurring. All the colours of him – his pink skin, his black hair, his green eyes, his red nose – all seemed to become incredibly bright, and brighter, and brighter, until there was an immense explosion of colour, sparks flying all around him, as if he'd exploded. But the man was still unaware of anything happening.

Tommy heard Sally Anne's voice saying: "That explosion is how we – how can I explain? – tune into him. The ride gets a little rougher here, Tommy, so hold on to your seat a little tighter now." Then he heard her laugh as if this was all a game!

Tommy looked again at the man. He seemed to be younger. He had originally looked as if he was about thirty-five, but now he was about twenty-five. He had a different suit on, a brighter one.

But now he seemed to be getting even younger again, right in front of Tommy's eyes.

Tommy blinked and the man was now a boy of about his own age. Tommy was trying not to blink now in case he missed anything.

Now he was a toddler.

Now he was a baby. Tommy couldn't keep up with the pace. He heard a slight boom and the baby seemed to explode in bright colours.

Now there was just dust. It cleared to reveal a man in a German soldier's uniform from World War II!

But still he was getting younger but at a much quicker pace than before. It was almost like watching a blur, constantly changing – another boom and the soldier was now a sailor from what looked like Nelson's time.

Boom. Now he was a child dressed in rags from Shakespeare's time. All the time the man was changing, his skin was stretching and shrinking, his face was growing larger, getting smaller, all at such a pace.

Sally Anne's voice then said: "Look around the carriage."

All the people in the carriage were undergoing the same transformations. All their past lives were flashing before Tommy's eyes!

All of a sudden, the train stopped with a jolt. Now, instead of the people in the carriage just sitting down, they all seemed to get up and start acting out all their past lives' important experiences!

The men who had been soldiers in past lives were covered in blood. Tommy could see them getting hit by bullets. He saw them contort their faces in pain. He heard them scream.

He saw other men, fighting with swords, as if they were from the days of pirates. He saw the swords entering flesh as the pirates fought each other to the death. All these horrific scenes were going on all at once. All changing instantly into other scenes as the past lives of the other passengers on the train unfolded before Tommy's eyes.

The scenes were so real. He could smell the sea, the fields, the blood, everything. It was getting too much for him. He had his eyes closed but remarkably it made no difference – he could still see it all. He put his hands over his ears – but he could still hear it all. He screamed, but nothing changed. Even with his eyes shut, he could see that the other passengers, all in some terrible scenes from past lives, heard his scream.

The pirates grinned and started walking towards him. The soldiers pointed their rifles at him.

They all were screaming at him, their voices filled with hate. Ugly faces, contorted in pain and in fear, were only feet away when he heard Sally Anne's voice say, "Shout 'to the end of your life!' to them. Quickly, Tommy!"

Tommy, without hesitating, shouted: "To the end of your life!"

All the horrible creatures from the passengers' past lives exploded at that very instant. Bits of them flew against the windows, chairs, doors – everywhere was splattered in blood.

Just then, the train jolted forward. Tommy blinked. When his eyes reopened, it was as if nothing had happened. He was breathless and panting. One or two of the other passengers, now all looking completely normal, looked around at him. Then they carried on reading their papers, chatting or just looking out the window.

Sally Anne was looking at him, concerned.

Again, the only noise to be heard was the sound of the train moving along the line.

Tommy looked out the window. It was daylight. Bright, sunny daylight! But when he and Sally Anne had boarded the train, it was nine o'clock, dark and raining.

"Are you all right?" he heard Sally Anne ask.

"Am I meant to be after that?" asked Tommy.

"That depends."

"On what?"

"On how determined you are to sort out your past," she said.

"After that, very determined!" he said, at last, utterly convinced that he was in the grip of forces more powerful than himself.

"Well, in that case, you'll be all right."

"I'm relieved to hear it!"

Tommy sat there thinking furiously. Maybe it was a trick. No. No way. It was too real. Every time a doubt crept into his mind, he just needed to look out the window at the broad daylight at – he checked his watch – 9.45pm.

The train pulled into Rolwell station and all the passengers rose from their seats. As usual, there was some slight pushing as the passengers tried to

squeeze down the narrow aisle. Tommy acciden-
tally bumped into the man that Sally Anne had first
pointed to – the man across the carriage who'd been
looking out of the window. In this minor collision,
the man dropped the newspaper he'd been holding.
Tommy bent down and picked it up.

"Danke schon," said the man, who immediately corrected himself and said, in broken English,
"Thank you."

He smiled and re-folded the newspaper.
Tommy could see it was called *Der Speigel* which he
knew was a German newspaper. This was the man
who, if Tommy's strange vision earlier had been
true, had been a German soldier in a past life.

If Tommy had any doubts before, they were
all gone now.

He whispered tentatively to Sally Anne as they
stepped onto the platform: "Were my past lives as
eventful as these ones you just showed me?"

"Yes. Oh, yes. That's why we're here," she
said ominously.

Chapter 14

"Come and meet my family," said Sally Anne as they walked away from the station.

"Why do I feel like I'm on the way to meet the Addams family?" Tommy said quietly.

They'd walked for some time until they came to the gate of a beautiful large old house. It was detached. There were other similar houses nearby.

They walked up the path together and Sally Anne produced a key from her pocket to unlock the door.

"I live here with many relatives. I like big families, don't you?" she asked.

"Depends on the family," replied Tommy. "I

know some families that I wish were much smaller!"

As they walked through the hallway of Sally Anne's home, Tommy wondered where everybody was.

"They are out at work," said Sally Anne, reading his mind again. She smiled and said, "Coffee?"

She told Tommy to sit down at the breakfast bar in the kitchen. He did. Then he said: "No. No coffee. Let's get to the point."

"Well," she said looking at him kindly, "You're as ready as you'll ever be!"

She sat opposite him and said: "Are you sure you're not thirsty or hungry? This may take some time."

"No. The quicker we start, the quicker we'll finish," said Tommy, not rudely, but matter-of-fact.

"How logical. Okay then. Here goes. I am a white witch. That means I have what people foolishly call supernatural powers. These powers are in fact, very natural and we were all born with them many, many thousands of years ago. But, while we evolved as humans, the spiritual side of our nature regressed. In other words, the better we got physically, the worse we got spiritually."

"Hold on," said Tommy. "That's a lot of big words."

"How come? You know what a spirit is don't you?"

"Yes."

"Well then. Of course you understand. Anyway, my story – or should I say - our story started in Ancient Egypt . . ."

"I've got to say slow down. Take me along slowly. This is still incredible to take in," pleaded Tommy.

"You were a prince. I was a servant girl. You treated me kindly when everyone else treated me cruelly. I promised you when you died, that I'd always help you in your future lives."

"How did I die?" asked Tommy.

"Your father, the King and his court, had you put to death because you wouldn't let them put me to death. They said I was a sorcerer – which was true. But, as I've said, I was a white witch. That means I only use my powers to help people."

"I know what a white witch is . . ."

"So, you tried to explain that I was helping people but this they took great offence at."

"Why?"

"Because I was a servant – low class. How dare I offer to help Kings? And of course, they were frightened by my powers. The King wasn't a bad man for his times. He knew you'd live again. But, these were bad times. You were traumatised by the fact your own father ordered your death. The night before they killed you, we talked all night. You were in a dungeon. But I visited you in spirit. You were terrified. I promised always to be with you."

Tommy sat in stunned silence. Tears were sliding down his silent face. She wiped them. Then she kissed him.

He felt himself relax, deeply. He felt as if he was drifting out of his body. In a moment, he was in the sky with the stars – he seemed to be flying. He felt the cold air, the swoosh of his own speed as he effortlessly drifted over continents that looked like tiny stains below him. He felt the pull of the earth as he was dragged down. In an instant, he was in a dark, clay dungeon. It was small and stuffy with just a stick with a flame at the end – an ancient torch – hanging somehow on the wall.

He smelled smells he hadn't smelled for thousands of years and yet he felt as if he'd never been away from this lonely dim cell. He felt fear rise within him. Then he had a vision of Sally Anne. She was telling him that everything would be all right, that there was an afterlife.

"No there isn't," he heard himself say.

"There is, you've got to believe me. We'll meet again. You've saved me. So I'll save you."

He felt doubt. But he seemed to be aware of more than this. It was as if he was trying to tell himself that he knew for sure there was an afterlife.

Gradually, fear left him. The torch on the wall burned lower. A door opened. Two rough men in Egyptian clothes took hold of him and dragged him out. He didn't struggle. He just smiled. He knew for sure that he would see the servant girl again. He knew she would save him. If not this time, then in some other world, some other time. Then he seemed to feel tremendous pain all over. But instantly, it was gone. Now he was in space again. Unfearful, dreaming, drifting, remembering that he was Tommy McDonald, soon to be award-winning journalist, but now one not afraid of the past!

He felt a kiss on his lips. He opened his eyes, as if they'd been shut! Sally Anne pulled back and smiled across the breakfast bar at him.

"Sally Anne – I – I don't know what to say – this is incredible. Me? A prince?"

"Well, not now Tommy," she said, trying to bring him back to earth. "You were once, long ago. We've all had our great moments in history. But that's not the point. We've got to remember what scared us most. Fear stops us developing. We have to confront our greatest fear . . ."

"You mean like spiders?" interrupted Tommy.
"What!"
"I'm scared of spiders, all bugs in fact . . ."

"Excuse me, I'm trying to be all heavy and serious here," said Sally Anne.

"Okay, okay. Lets see if I've got this right. You are a witch."

"A white one," she reminded him.

"A white one. This I now believe. So why have you appeared to save me now?" he asked, teasingly. He was still curious as to why it had taken him thousands of years to be rescued.

"Because, you are a stubborn ox!" she said. "When the Romans were in Britain, you were too busy studying to be a great road engineer! You wouldn't believe who I was. When the Armada was being prepared in Spain to attack England, I was a gypsy traveller in Spanish villages. You were a young volunteer soldier, lying about your age to join the Spanish army. The scene from the picture I painted in Mr Bush's class – that was the last time I made contact with you. You were a coal seller . . ."

"A coal cellar?"

"No, I mean you sold coal from a cart."

"But how come I don't remember?"

"Because every time, in every lifetime, I met you and "spooked you out" as you would say. We always got to the point of discovery and you would lose your nerve."

"Like tonight, before we got on the train?"

"That's right. You always were so practical. Always worried about the future. You didn't want to get involved in things that would interfere with your future. And yes, you were always successful, but your old age was always filled with regret."

"What was the difference this time then?" asked Tommy, confused.

"This time, I used more of my powers. This time I used magic, like on the train."

"Why didn't you use that before?" inquired Tommy.

"Because, every time I use my powers, it lessens them a little."

"You mean that my lack of faith has weakened you!" said Tommy worried.

"Yes," was the blunt, honest answer.

Tommy paused long and hard before eventually saying, "Sorry. I'm really sorry."

"You can make up for it by acknowledging that there is more to life than this life," said Sally Anne.

"Does that mean this life is not important – like it doesn't matter if I pass exams or do well?" said Tommy, suddenly enjoying the possibility that life could be a barrel load of fun without worry!

"Of course it matters. You have to try your best at whatever you do. Anything else is a waste of time – precious time. But remember that there is more. Anyway, I've told the story. Do you believe me?" she looked very insecure. She was frowning.

"Yes," said Tommy immediately. "Yes. Without any doubt. I recognise all the lives you've described."

"I hope so. Because you won't always remember," said Sally Anne.

"Why not? I'm not very likely to forget all this, am I?"

"Yes. And you'll wonder if it was all a dream."

"But you'll always be in school to remind me – won't you?" he asked.

"Even if I'm not, I'll be around. Somewhere." She looked at her watch.

"Come on," she said, "you'll miss the last train back."

"But there's so much to say – can't we talk some more . . ."

"You don't understand. The next train really is the last."

Tommy instinctively knew what she meant. It really would be the last train back.

"But we'll talk tomorrow, right?" he asked as they walked at pace towards the station.

"I might not be in tomorrow."

"Well, the next day – some time?"

She looked at him as he purchased his ticket and said, "Some time. Yes. Some time."

"Great. I can't wait," said Tommy, misunderstanding her, tragically.

Chapter 15

What was he going to say to his parents?

"Where have you been?" he imagined them saying. How could he reply that he had been to outer space, Ancient Egypt – oh, never mind he said to himself, this will be my secret. Our secret, he thought he heard Sally Anne's voice say.

"Okay," he replied out loud. "Our secret."

"Where have you been?" exclaimed his parents, one after the other, as he tried unsuccessfully to sneak in the front door.

"Out," he replied.

"Thank you. That really clears up that mystery then, doesn't it," said his angry mother.

Just then the phone rang.

"Hello!" said Mrs McDonald, annoyed that her inquisition had been interrupted. There was a pause as Mr McDonald listened.

"Oh . . . I see . . . okay then Mrs Dickens . . . yes . . . thank you for phoning." She put down the phone.

"Who was that?" asked Mr McDonald.

"That was Mrs Dickens, Sally Anne's mother."

"Oh, the old girlfriend's mother," said Mr McDonald, now smiling. "So that's where he's been. On a date?"

"Helping her with homework, according to Mrs Dickens," Tommy's mother looked suspiciously at him.

"Yeah," said Tommy, grasping the lifeline that Sally Anne's mother had thrown him. "That's right. She's the new girl. The classwork is a little ahead of her so I'm helping her. I really was."

Mrs McDonald looked relieved.

"We thought you'd joined a gang or something. Up to no good. I don't believe for a minute you were doing just homework – is this girl pretty?"

"Oh, I . . . err . . . haven't really noticed," said Tommy blushing.

Mum and Dad burst out laughing.

As he was walking up the stair, his mum shouted up: "But no more secrets, young man. Do you hear me?"

"Yes," he replied, saying to himself :"That will be right!"

Chapter 16

Sally Anne wasn't at school the next day. Miss Sharpe said it turned out that Sally Anne's dad had got another job, better than the one he'd taken in this area.

Tommy was not surprised. He'd mulled it over in his head all night. She'd done her bit. The rest was now up to him.

"Shame about Sally Anne," said George at lunch time.

"Yeah."

"Life goes on though, eh?"

"Yeah, that's for sure."

"So, did you kiss her?" asked George, determined to discover the really important secrets Tommy was hiding.

"Yeah, as a matter of fact, I did."

"Yes!" shouted George to all the playground. "Tommy McDonald has scored a point at long last!"

"Four times."

"A point AND goal difference! You've really grown up at last!" exclaimed George.

"Countless times," replied Tommy.

Chapter 17

Out of curiosity, Tommy went to the school library after his last class. He was looking for a map of the whole area. He found one. He had an idea that he wouldn't find what he was looking for. And he didn't. He was looking for Rolwell, Sally Anne's home. His home town, she'd said. But he knew that was just a phoney bit of spice to get him to go there. Nowhere on the map did it mention Rolwell. It didn't exist. He wasn't worried.

That night, he went to the train station. He looked at all the destinations. Rolwell wasn't on the board. Or in the timetables. No railway staff had heard of it. He wasn't surprised.

On the way out of the station, he saw a man at the taxi queue reading a foreign newspaper. It was called *Der Speigel*. Tommy recognised the man. The man, as he folded his paper to get into a taxi, caught Tommy's eye.

"Don't lose your train ticket," he called out to Tommy. "You might want to help someone one day."

The taxi disappeared around a corner.

"My ticket?" Tommy wondered. Then he searched in his jeans pocket. He pulled out a crumpled bit of paper. It said, on the destination part of the ticket, very clearly, Rolwell.

Many times, in the years to come, Tommy wondered whether he'd had a nervous breakdown or something around the Sally Anne time. George and he remained friends for years and rarely spoke of Sally Anne. They never discussed the mysterious side of the affair. Mr Bush, at the end of that term, threw out all the pupils' artwork, so Tommy never even got the chance to examine Sally Anne's painting again.

But, whenever he'd convinced himself that he had imagined the whole thing, he went to the top drawer of his desk in his bedroom and pulled out the train ticket. That's what kept it all real in his head.

He still dreamed about Sally Anne and she told him in these dreams that she was happy. Because he believed the whole story, and he did, she was able to regain all her witch's strength and continue to help others, lost in time.

Tommy still worked hard, but he lived for the present. He still worried sometimes about the future, but he never again worried about the past.

We hope you have enjoyed this story from the pen of Edgar J. Hyde. Here are some other titles in the Creepers series for you to collect:

Rag & Bone Man
Payback Time
Noisy Neighbours
Pen Pals
The Sold Souls

This series was conceived by Edgar J. Hyde and much of the text was provided by his minions, under slavish conditions and pain of death! Thankfully, none of these minions defied their master and so we can say 'thank you' to them for toughing it out and making this series possible.

Edgar J. Hyde, however, has yet more plans for these dungeon-bound slaves. "No rest for the wicked" is his motto!

Creepers

RAG & BONE MAN

In a small village the night after every funeral, an apparition of a Rag and Bone man, with his horse and cart, reputedly makes his way down the high street.

The trouble is, the person reporting the sight is normally the next person in a coffin!

Thus a conspiracy of silence prevails among the locals and the legend remains unconfirmed. Until, after the death of an elderly relative, Bryan Codie and Dave decide to investigate . . .

Creepers

THE
SOLD SOULS

A collection of overambitious high school children who, through dabbling in the occult, sell their souls to a harmless, minor demon who poses as the Devil! They would do anything for success, not knowing that by selling their souls to an impostor, they have incurred the wrath of the real thing!

Now the real Devil gets his own back by posing convincingly as people they know. They are then led, in blissful ignorance to untimely ends.

Will any of them survive?

Creepers

NOISY NEIGHBOURS

A seemingly puritanically-minded family move to a big run-down area in a big city.

They refuse to talk to their new neighbours as they regard them as inferior. But something doesn't quite fit with this family. At night all the wild, partying noises come from their house and through the blinds, the neighbours see shadows of what looks like inhuman forms.

Killjoys during the day – fun lovers at night, this Jekyll and Hyde type family come under the scrutiny of three teenage would-be ghost busters!

Creepers

PAYBACK TIME

A family's life is made a misery by loansharks who then discover that they have bitten off more than they can chew. The family pay back the moneylenders in carefully worked out instalments and with interest!

Mysteriously, the family is helped by the sympathetic previous tenant of their home, who was forced out by the same loansharks in the past

This tenant disappeared under unexplained circumstances and now seems to appear only at the moments of most need!

Creepers

PEN PALS

Olivia and Natasha are best friends who sometimes write notes to each other for fun.

These notes start to contain suggestions that are not their own. Someone has a warning for Olivia. It appears that someone, somehow, has a message to convey. A ghostly warning that someone the schoolgirls think of as a friend is not to be trusted

If only they knew which one . . .